LEO & DIANE DILLON

Mother Goose

Numbers on the Loose

HARCOURT, INC.

Orlando Austin New York

San Diego Toronto London

MANUFACTURED IN CHINA

A NOTE FROM THE ILLUSTRATORS

For generations the rhymes of Mother Goose have been offered to young children as an invitation to language, to books, and most of all, to the imagination. Here we offer children an invitation to numbers as well, to playful, energetic, magical, even at times mischievous numbers—numbers on the loose.

As we began to gather verses for the collection, we wondered if we would find enough number rhymes for a whole book. But as we read through old volumes from the early twentieth century, our problem quickly became one of selecting from among too many choices. We decided that we wanted our collection to include both well- and lesser-known rhymes, to progress from rhymes with smaller numbers to those with larger numbers, and most importantly, that we wanted our volume to honor the wonderful, fantastical quality of Mother Goose. We found ourselves imagining a clock with not only hands but also arms with which to ring itself, fish who row boats, and masked characters who can be whatever they choose in a world where everyone belongs.

We have used versions of the rhymes we found in the early twentieth-century collections we consulted, but Mother Goose is an oral tradition, and variations abound. Knowing there is no one definitive text, we have even taken two small liberties of our own: making the child in "Baa, baa, black sheep" a girl and rewarding the barber who shaves the pig with a powder puff rather than a pinch of snuff. Like the numbers—and like Mother Goose herself—we have allowed ourselves to be on the loose!

1, 2, 3,
The bumblebee,
The rooster crows
And away he goes.

WASH the dishes,
Wipe the dishes,
Ring the bell for tea;
3 good wishes,
3 good kisses,
I will give to thee.

BAA, baa, black sheep,
Have you any wool?
Yes, sir, yes, sir,
3 bags full:

1 for the master,
And **1** for the dame,
And **1** for the little girl
Who lives down the lane.

CHARLEY Barley, butter and eggs,
Sold his wife for **3** duck eggs.
When the ducks began to lay
Charley Barley flew away.

EARLY in the morning at **8** o'clock
You can hear the postman's knock;
Up jumps Ella to answer the door,
1 letter, **2** letters, **3** letters, **4**!

THERE were **2** wrens upon a tree,
Whistle and I'll come to thee.
Another came, and there were **3**,
Whistle and I'll come to thee.

Another came and there were **4**.
You needn't whistle anymore,
For being frightened, off they flew,
And there are none to show to you.

1st in a carriage,
2nd in a gig,

3rd on a donkey,
And 4th on a pig.

1, 2, 3, 4, 5,
Catching fishes all alive.
Why did you let them go?

Because they bit my finger so.
Which finger did they bite?
The little finger on the right.

1 for anger,
2 for mirth,
3 for a wedding,
4 for a birth,

5 for rich,
6 for poor,
7 for a witch,
I can tell you no more.

1 potato, 2 potato,
3 potato, 4,
5 potato, 6 potato,
7 potato, more.
O-U-T spells out,
So out you must go,
Because the king and queen say so.

1, 2, 3, 4,
Mary at the cottage door;
5, 6, 7, 8,
Eating cherries off a plate.
O-U-T spells out!

1, 2, 3, 4, 5,
I caught a hare alive;

6, 7, 8, 9, 10,
let him go again.

HICKETY, pickety, my black hen,
She lays eggs for gentlemen;
Sometimes **9**, and sometimes **1O**,
Hickety, pickety, my black hen.

1, 2,
Buckle my shoe;

3, 4,
Knock at the door;

5, 6,
Pick up sticks;

7, 8,
Lay them straight;

9, 10,
A good fat hen.

1-ery, 2-ery, tickery, 10,
Bobs of vinegar, gentlemen.
A bird in the air,

A fish in the sea,
A bonny wee lassie
Came singing to me.

CHOOK, chook, chook, chook, chook,
Good morning, Mrs. Hen,
How many chickens have you got?
Madam, I've got **10.**
4 of them are yellow,
And **4** of them are brown,
And **2** of them are speckled red,
The nicest in the town.

3 young rats with black felt hats,
3 young ducks with white straw flats,
3 young dogs with curling tails,
3 young cats with demi-veils,

Went out to walk with **2** young pigs
In satin vests and sorrel wigs.
But suddenly it chanced to rain
And so they all went home again.

FROM Wibbleton to Wobbleton is **15** miles,
From Wobbleton to Wibbleton is **15** miles,

From Wibbleton to Wobbleton,
From Wobbleton to Wibbleton,
From Wibbleton to Wobbleton
is **15** miles.

HICKERY, dickery,
6 and **7**,

Alabone, crackabone,
10 and **11**,

Spin, spun,
Muskidun,

Twiddle 'em,
Twaddle 'em,
21.

BARBER, barber, shave a pig;
How many hairs will make a wig?

4-and-20, that's enough;
Give the barber a powder puff.

SING a song of sixpence,
A pocket full of rye;
4-and-20 blackbirds
Baked in a pie;

When the pie was open'd,
The birds began to sing;
Was not that a dainty dish,
To set before a king?

The king was in his counting-house
Counting out his money;
The queen was in the parlor
Eating bread and honey.

The maid was in the garden
Hanging out the clothes,
When there came a little blackbird
And snapped off her nose.

GREGORY Griggs, Gregory Griggs,
Had **27** different wigs.
He wore them up, he wore them down,
To please the people of the town;

He wore them east, he wore them west,
But he never could tell which he loved best.

LITTLE Blue Ben, who lives in the glen,
Keeps a blue cat and **1** blue hen,

Which lays of blue eggs a score and **10.**
Where shall I find the little Blue Ben?

THERE were **2** blackbirds sitting on a hill,
1 named Jack and the other named Jill.
Fly away, Jack! Fly away, Jill!
Come again, Jack! Come again, Jill!

Requests for permission to make copies of any part of the
work should be submitted online at www.harcourt.com/contact
or mailed to the following address: Permissions Department,
Harcourt, Inc., 6277 Sea Harbor Drive, Orlando,
Florida 32887-6777.

www.HarcourtBooks.com

Library of Congress Cataloging-in-Publication Data
Dillon, Leo.
Mother Goose numbers on the loose/
by Leo and Diane Dillon.
p.   cm.
Summary: Presents an illustrated collection of twenty-four
counting rhymes, from "Baa, baa black sheep" to
"Wash the dishes, wipe the dishes."
1. Nursery rhymes.   2. Children's poetry.
3. Counting-out rhymes.   [1. Nursery rhymes.   2. Counting.]
I. Dillon, Diane, ill.   II. Title.
PZ8.3.D585Mot   2007
398.8'4—dc22   2005037763
ISBN 978-0-15-205676-6

H G F E D

The illustrations in this book were done in gouache
on watercolor paper, with touches of pencil.
The display type was set in Zephyr.
The text type was set in Xavier Serif-Medium.
Color separations by Bright Arts Ltd., Hong Kong
Manufactured by South China Printing Company, Ltd., China
Production supervision by Pascha Gerlinger
Designed by Scott Piehl and April Ward

For Anne,
who was the inspiration for this book

And for the teachers,
who keep the numbers in line

—L. D. & D. D.